THE SCHOOL LIBRARY DISASTER

by
JACQUELINE PINTO

Illustrated by Trevor Stubley

HAMISH HAMILTON
LONDON

First published in Great Britain 1986
by Hamish Hamilton Children's Books
Garden House   57–59 Long Acre   London WC2E 9JZ
Text copyright © 1986 by Jacqueline Pinto
Illustrations copyright © 1986 by Trevor Stubley

British Library Cataloguing in Publication Data
Pinto, Jacqueline
   The school library disaster.—(Antelope books)
   I. Title   II. Stubley, Trevor
   823'.914[J]   PZ7
   ISBN 0–241–11776–3

Filmset in Baskerville by
Typeset by Katerprint Co. Ltd, Oxford
Printed in Great Britain at the
University Press, Cambridge

Chapter 1

DARREN DRAKE AND his friends knew they weren't allowed to run along the school corridors . . . but they often forgot.

Every time, however, they were caught by Miss Wilson, their class teacher. She would be very cross indeed and would tell them that they MUST OBEY SCHOOL RULES.

One Monday morning, Darren, Mike Sinclair and Jim Harvey ran into school and then chased each other all the way down the corridor to their classroom. When they got there, they suddenly realised that Miss Wilson hadn't come along to stop them.

The boys couldn't understand it. Not once, since their first day at Redwood Primary School, had that happened.

"Perhaps Miss Wilson woke up late and is still eating her breakfast," said Darren. He thought it would be a nice change if Miss Wilson did something wrong instead of them.

"Or else she thinks it's Saturday and won't come to school at all," suggested Jim hopefully.

By now several other boys and girls had come into the classroom. Among them were Sarah Moore, Lucy Farmer and Jyoti Patel. They had some news for Class Three because they had met Mr Page in the entrance hall.

"Mr Page says we must all go into Assembly as soon as we hear the bell," said Sarah. "He's got a special announcement to make."

"Not another one!" groaned Darren. "What have we done this time?"

Mr Page's "special announcements" usually meant trouble for someone . . . and that someone was usually from Class Three.

Mr Page was the headmaster of Redwood. He was a short man and was rather fat. Normally he smiled a lot and was very good tempered, but every now and then something would upset him. Then his face would go bright red and he would wave his arms around as he spoke. When that happened, the boys and girls at Redwood stopped talking and did exactly what he said. Otherwise they were afraid he might explode!

When the bell rang for Assembly and Class Three filed into their place at the back of the hall, they expected to see Miss Wilson up on the platform with

Mr Page. As well as being their class teacher, she was also the deputy head and was never absent from school.

To their surprise she wasn't there.

It wasn't long before Mr Page came to his "special announcement". In a loud voice, he said, "Miss Wilson will be away from school for four weeks on a special course but I have arranged for a supply teacher to take her place. Her name is Miss Edwards."

He went on speaking very slowly and sternly. "As soon as Assembly is over, Class Three should go back to their room and wait for Miss Edwards to arrive. NOW I DON'T WANT TO HEAR ANY NOISE COMING FROM THAT CLASSROOM. DO YOU ALL UNDERSTAND?"

Mr Page glared at every member of the class but his eyes rested longest on Darren.

Darren took the hint. He decided he wouldn't make the slightest sound until the new teacher appeared.

He and the rest of Class Three almost crept back to their room and went straight to their desks. Five minutes went by, then another five minutes. There was no sign of Miss Edwards.

Darren wondered if she had got lost. "We can't sit like this all morning," he said. "I'm getting pins and needles."

Frank Randall (whose dad was a dentist) was the class expert on medical matters. "My grandpa says it's bad for your heart to stay still for too long," he declared in a warning voice.

Mike remembered Mr Page's words. "What else can we do if we can't make any noise?"

Darren had a bright idea. "If we play shipwrecks *very quietly*, Mr Page won't be able to hear us."

"What's shipwrecks?" asked Jyoti. She hadn't been at Redwood for long, and she had never heard of this game.

Mike explained. "You've got to get round the room without letting your feet touch the floor. If they do, you're drowned!"

Jyoti still looked puzzled as the boys and girls moved the desks and chairs around. They arranged them so that they could just jump from one to another without falling into the imaginary sea.

Darren appointed himself captain of the big ship that suddenly struck an iceberg. "Quick, everyone," he announced in a booming voice. "Water's coming in! We'll have to escape. I'll lead the way."

Lucy, who liked arguing with Darren, said at once, "You can't be the first to leave a sinking ship. *Real* captains have to stay behind and make sure the women and children get away."

Darren glared at her. The trouble with Lucy was that she was often right. "You go first, then," he growled, "but don't blame me if you fall in."

"Of course I shan't," said Lucy indignantly. She was the best in her class at games and gym. She scrambled

on to her desk, jumped across to the
nearest chair, then clung to the big
wooden bookshelves as she made her
way carefully along the wide bottom
shelf.

The others followed more slowly.
They weren't as agile as Lucy. Sarah
was the worst. She managed to get from
the desk to the chair but when it came

to the bookshelves she simply had to put her foot down on the floor to steady herself.

"YOU'RE OUT!" yelled Darren. "You're in the water! You've drowned!"

Sarah managed to heave herself on to

the bookshelves. "No, I haven't!" she shouted back.

"YES, YOU HAVE!" screamed out several of the others.

In the commotion, no one heard footsteps outside.

Suddenly the door was flung open and Mr Page came marching in. He stopped in amazement as he saw them all on top of the desks and chairs. His face went red and he shouted, "WHAT ARE YOU DOING? DIDN'T I TELL YOU TO BE QUIET?"

Darren looked unhappy. "I'm sorry, Mr Page," he said, and he really meant it. In the excitement of the game, they had all forgotten about keeping quiet.

Luckily for Class Three, Mr Page had a special reason for not spending any more time with them. Besides this, standing just behind him was the new teacher. He had brought her along to introduce her to the class, and he didn't want her to start off with any unpleasantness.

"This is Miss Edwards," he said in an icy tone. "She will be looking after you until Miss Wilson returns. Now put all the desks back and sit down on your chairs and DON'T EVER CLIMB ON SCHOOL PROPERTY AGAIN!"

Mr Page stepped aside to let the new teacher come in. He then left the room without saying another word.

Miss Edwards walked over to the blackboard and turned to face them. "Come on, now, you heard what Mr Page said. What are you waiting for?" she asked gently.

There was absolute silence in the room. Everyone just stared at her and gaped.

Their new teacher was not a bit like Miss Wilson. Miss Edwards was young and slim and very pretty. Her hair was a mass of curls, her face was soft and smooth-looking and her eyes were the colour of the blue hyacinths which were flowering on the nature table. Besides all that, she was wearing a lovely fluffy yellow top and a flowery skirt.

Darren, who never noticed what people looked like, was quite overcome.

Mike couldn't take his eyes off her.

Lucy wondered if she could persuade her mum to buy her a fluffy yellow top and flowery skirt.

Chapter 2

THE REASON WHY Mr Page had been in such a hurry to leave the scene of the shipwreck was that he had an appointment with Mrs Farmer, whose daughter, Lucy, was in Class Three.

Lucy's mum was a determined lady who was always brimming over with ideas. Sometimes her ideas were no good at all, but every now and then she had one that hit the jackpot.

As soon as Mr Page arrived back in his office, slightly flushed from his encounter with Class Three, his secretary came in to tell him that Mrs Farmer and Mrs Henderson (the president of the Parents and Teachers Association) had arrived.

The two ladies followed her in, settled themselves down on the chairs opposite Mr Page and came straight to the point.

Mrs Henderson spoke first. "Mrs Farmer has had *another* good idea." Then, seeing the worried look on the headmaster's face, she added reassuringly, "It's all right. This is a very good idea. I think you will like it."

Mrs Farmer took a deep breath and began speaking. "I've thought for a long time—and now Mrs Henderson and several other parents in the P.T.A. agree with me—that Redwood School should have a proper library." She paused for a moment to see what effect this suggestion would have on Mr Page.

He looked surprised. "We have bookshelves in each classroom and we have a good selection of books already."

Mrs Farmer gave a disapproving sniff. "That's not what I call a library. Besides, some of the books are old and some are very tatty! No, I'm talking about a PROPER library . . . a room which is kept just for that purpose . . . with bookshelves round the walls . . . and tables and chairs where the children can sit and read quietly without being disturbed."

For a moment, Mr Page was taken aback. He couldn't think off-hand of any boys and girls in his school who would want to sit quietly without being disturbed. Then he pulled himself together and said, "Well, it is a good idea but it's one that will cost a lot of money. Books are very expensive . . . "

Mrs Henderson interrupted him.

"Ah, but this is where the P.T.A. can help. Mrs Farmer and I have spoken to several parents and we all think we should have a school uniform sale— perhaps next Friday afternoon—in the Assembly Hall. The children grow out of their clothes so quickly and we would like the chance of buying good second-hand uniform. If we are able to *sell* the old uniform, we could keep some of the money and we could give the rest to a special library fund."

Mr Page suddenly gave a broad

smile. "What an EXCELLENT idea!" he exclaimed happily. "You can certainly use the Assembly Hall next Friday and I'll see if we can think of any other ideas for raising money at the sale. Yes, it's about time young Darren Drake and his gang wore proper uniform . . . Now, as far as the actual library is concerned, we have an empty room upstairs which will be ideal."

News always travelled fast at Redwood School. By the time dinner-break was over that day, everyone had heard about the new library and the school uniform sale. Mr Page also let it be known that he would welcome suggestions from the children for other ways of making money. This, he decided afterwards, was a mistake because he was overwhelmed with ideas . . . most of which were very silly.

There were, however, two which met with his approval. The oldest girl in the school suggested there should be a produce stall, with flowers and fruit and vegetables and tinned food from everyone's home. Mr Page was also pleased with Lucy's idea—a second-hand toy and book stall.

Class Three didn't entirely agree with Lucy. "No one will bring toys that are any good," declared Darren. "I know I wouldn't! There'll only be broken things or boring books that no one wants."

Jim thought Darren was making a fuss about nothing. "Well, it doesn't matter," he said, "just so long as we're not having to do any work." Jim had never been very keen on lessons. He liked games and going home much better.

Mike tried to be constructive. "Perhaps we can think of something else . . . "

Darren wrinkled his brow, pursed his lips and said nothing for a moment. Then inspiration struck. "I know," he said excitedly. "We can have a live animal stall!"

By now, the rest of the class had gathered round Darren's desk. Lucy was quick to snub Darren's idea. "We're not allowed to bring animals to school," she argued.

"But this is for a good cause," countered Darren. "Anyway, Pagey needn't know."

Jyoti Patel, whose dad owned the supermarket opposite the school, suddenly shouted out, "I can bring a gerbil. One of my dad's customers gave me a gerbil and my mum hates it and

24

wants me to give it away. She says it makes such a noise at night scuttling around the cage that it keeps her awake."

Darren's eyes lit up. "That'll be great!"

Sarah said, "We can have a raffle and the gerbil can be the prize. We'll make a lot of money that way."

Lucy didn't approve at all. "My

mum wouldn't let me have a gerbil and I wouldn't want one, anyway. They're horrid furry things and they make me shudder."

Darren gave her a contemptuous look. "Not everyone's as silly as you!"

Miss Edwards came in at that point, so Lucy had to content herself with sticking her tongue out at Darren.

Class Three found it difficult to concentrate on their lessons that afternoon because they were so excited about their stall.

All the following week they talked about nothing else but they were careful to keep it a secret—even from Miss Edwards.

Everyone in the class promised to provide something.

"It doesn't matter what it is—as long as it's alive," explained Darren.

"Supposing I find a maggot in an apple, shall I bring that along?" asked Lucy scornfully.

Her sarcasm was lost on Darren. "Yeah, great!" he replied with enthusiasm.

Sarah wrinkled up her nose. She didn't fancy having rotten apples on their stall. She thought she might try to catch a butterfly . . . or even find a bird's egg.

Mike was the most practical member of the class. "We'd better join our stall on to the toy stall," he said. "Then if we say we need an extra table, Mr Page will think we're bringing in more toys and he won't ask what we want it for."

Early in the week, Mr Page had a special meeting with the teachers. He told them that after Assembly on Friday morning, a group of parents from the P.T.A. would come in to put price labels on the goods. They had managed to borrow several clothes rails and coat hangers so that all the blazers, anoraks, raincoats, school shirts and dresses could be hung up tidily. Mr Bragg, the school caretaker, was going to help set things up, and also carry several large tables into the hall for the cardigans and pullovers and the rest of the clothes.

"We shall need at least two tables for the second-hand toy and book stall," Miss Edwards reminded Mr Page. "Class Three are very excited about it and they have promised to bring in all sorts of things to make a good display. I must say I find everyone in that class most helpful ... especially Darren Drake and his friends."

"Oh!" said Mr Page, looking a little

surprised. Of course he had known
Darren and his friends for far longer
than Miss Edwards had. "Make sure
you keep your eye on them," he warned
her. "It's when they offer to help that
you have to watch out!"

Chapter 3

AT LAST FRIDAY came. After Assembly, a steady stream of parents called at the school. Mrs Henderson and Mrs Farmer sat at a table in the entrance hall and made sure that all the second-hand clothes were marked for size, and priced. When this was done, they handed them over to some other parents who were helping to sort things out.

The sale was due to start at half-past-two. Miss Edwards told Class Three that they could take their books and toys to the Assembly Hall immediately after dinner and she would be there to help arrange the toy stall.

By the time dinner was over, however, there were so many tins of food,
and flowers and vegetables, and so
much fruit piled up outside the Assembly Hall that Miss Edwards was fully
occupied helping to carry it all inside
and arrange on the produce stall.

This suited Darren and his gang.
They were able to smuggle in all the
things they had found and cared for
during the past week.

There was so much activity in the Hall that no one paid any attention to Class Three and none of the teachers noticed the animal cage which Jyoti and Mike carried into the room. Most of the boys and girls had also brought some of their old games and books and they arranged these carefully round the cage so, from a distance, no one could see exactly what was on the table.

There was, indeed, a magnificent display of live animals for sale. There was a jam jar filled with muddy water in which some tadpoles were darting around, and there were match boxes containing beetles and spiders. Frank Randall had brought along several wood-lice which he had found underneath some big stones in his back yard.

Sarah had persuaded her mum to let her have some lettuce leaves and also

some silver foil trays which she used in her freezer. On each tray Sarah had put a lettuce leaf and on top of that a nice, fat slithery worm. One of the other girls had found some caterpillars, and Jim had managed to catch a frog! He had taken his wet flannel from the bathroom that morning and had put it in the bottom of a shoe-box and had made some air holes in the lid. He said this was a much better home for the frog than the slimy pond in his garden. And there was the star prize—the gerbil, for the lucky raffle winner.

By now the parents were beginning to arrive. They were all dead keen to stock up with school uniform and as soon as they were let into the Assembly Hall they made a frantic rush for the tables. They went from the blazers and raincoats to the skirts and trousers,

then to the blouses and pullovers . . . then back again to the beginning to make sure they hadn't missed any bargains!

At first neither the teachers nor the parents paid any attention to the second-hand toy stall, which was at the far end of the Assembly Hall. The clothing and food stalls were keeping them busy enough.

Then the parents began to complain to the teachers that their children kept on disappearing and had to be dragged back from the toy stall to try on the clothes.

At that point Mr Page realised that something must be going on at the toy stall . . . even from the distance he could see the girls and boys were all pushing forward trying to get to the front.

He strode over to the far end of the Hall and stood at the edge of the crowd. For a few moments, he just watched and said nothing.

Then he sighed. He might have guessed. Darren and his gang were up to something. Why else would they be standing in front of the stall, shouting out instructions, collecting money, handing over bits of paper, then taking them back again before screwing them up and putting them in a large box?

"What is going on here?" he demanded.

No one heard. He asked again IN A VERY LOUD VOICE.

This time, everyone in the Hall heard and there was total silence.

Darren, flushed with excitement, was eager to explain. "We're collecting masses of money, Mr Page. If you give

us 5p, we'll let you have a piece of paper and you can write your name on it. Then we'll screw it up and put it in this box. We're going to ask someone to pick out one of the pieces of paper. The person whose name is on it will win the prize."

Everyone in Class Three looked at Mr Page. They were surprised that he wasn't looking more pleased . . . in fact he was actually GLARING at them all.

"What is the prize?" he asked in an icy voice.

"A gerbil!" shouted out Jyoti Patel. "My mum wanted me to get rid of it because she said it kept her awake at night. It's the very best thing on our table."

Jim asked politely, "Would you like

to buy a ticket, Mr Page? You might win the gerbil."

Mr Page did not answer. Then his face went very red and he began to wave his arms around. He looked as though he was about to EXPLODE.

But, of course, he didn't.

Class Three eyed him warily. Judging by the colour of his face, they knew something had displeased him.

Darren wondered if Mr Page was cross because he hadn't been asked to draw the prize. "Perhaps *you'd* like to pick out the winner?" he suggested, thinking this might put things right.

By now several parents had gathered round. Mrs Henderson said enthusiastically, "How *clever* of Class Three to have thought of raising money this way for the new library! Yes, *do* pick out the winning ticket, Mr Page."

Seeing all the parents' smiling faces, Mr Page knew that this was the moment for him to simmer down. He avoided looking at the squiggly worms and the grey wood-lice and the big black beetles and the long-legged spiders. He plunged his hand into the box of tickets, picked one out and unfolded it. He hesitated a moment before reading out the name.

All the boys and girls held their breath. Who was going to be the lucky prize winner?

"Darren Drake," said Mr Page, trying to muster up a smile.

Everyone cheered. Darren beamed from ear to ear. He had wanted that gerbil from the very moment he set eyes on it. "Thank you," he said happily.

Mr Page reached out for the cage and handed it to Darren, saying sternly as

he did so, "YOU MUST NOT BRING
THIS GERBIL INTO SCHOOL
AGAIN!"

Darren promised faithfully that he
wouldn't—and he really *meant* to keep
his promise.

Chapter 4

ON MONDAY MORNING, Mr Page smiled at everyone as they filed into Assembly. He was delighted with the whole school. The teachers, the parents and all the boys and girls had worked really hard to make the sale a success. As a result, much more money had been raised than either he or the P.T.A. had expected.

"As a reward for your great effort," he said during his announcements, "I am going to take ten boys and girls from each class to the bookshop in Applegate to help choose some new books for our library."

43

Class Three had to wait till Thursday for their turn. Miss Edwards found it difficult to decide who should be the lucky ten because they *all* wanted to go. Eventually she chose Darren, Mike, Jim, Sarah and Jyoti because they had worked the hardest at the sale. She also chose Lucy Farmer, Frank Randall and three others because they were the best at reading.

As well as Mr Page, there was to be one parent from each class going on the trip. Mrs Farmer said that she would like to be there as the new library was her idea. Lucy was pleased. She liked having her mum around.

Darren was not so pleased. He and Lucy always argued with each other, but if her mum was there, she'd be sure to tell him to stop.

On Thursday morning, Darren

44

arrived early at school. Before he went inside, however, he hurried round to a shed in the playground where some of the games equipment was kept. He carefully put a cardboard box right at the back of the shed.

Immediately after Assembly, the chosen ten from Class Three were told to go straight to the minibus which Mr Bragg had parked outside school. While the others were lining up to climb in, Darren nipped round to the shed, picked up his cardboard box and hurried back to join the queue.

"What've you got in that box?" demanded Lucy. Her sharp eyes saw everything.

Darren pretended not to hear. He didn't want Lucy to know his secret.

Darren went to a seat at the back of the minibus, put the box on the floor and held it firmly between his feet throughout the journey. Just before the minibus lurched to a stop outside the bookshop, Darren carefully opened the lid of the box, put his hand inside, lifted something out and put it in his blazer pocket.

Mr Page said they could have fifteen

minutes by themselves looking round the bookshop, then they should come back to the front of the shop with their suggestions. He gave each of them a pencil and a piece of paper so they could make a note of the author and the title of any book which they would like to have in the school library.

Everyone wandered around happily. There was a wonderful display of colourful picture books on every subject imaginable, as well as a big selection of story books.

Darren, Mike and Jim went to the far end of the shop where all the paperbacks were kept.

At first Lucy and Sarah and Jyoti stayed with the main group. Mr Page and Mrs Farmer were with them and they kept taking books down from the shelves and making suggestions as to which would be the most suitable for the library.

After a while, Lucy and Sarah and Jyoti decided they would see what Darren and Mike and Jim were doing, so they went to look for them at the back of the shop.

"Have you found anything?" asked Sarah as she saw the boys leafing through a book called *Barmy Bill in Outer Space*.

"My mum says we should have some more reference books," said Lucy in a disapproving voice.

Darren was indignant. "Mr Page said we could choose the books *we* want to read. Anyway, last time I took a reference book home from the library, I thought it was boring. My dog thought so, too, because he started to chew it— and then left half of it."

Lucy loved saying things to annoy Darren. "If you gave your dog *proper* food," she declared, "it wouldn't want to eat your books."

Darren was about to say something really rude when he had an idea . . . a brilliant idea . . .

He put his hand into his blazer pocket and brought out his gerbil. This was the secret that he had kept from Lucy.

When Lucy turned away to look at some other books, Darren put the gerbil on her shoulder.

The gerbil was so light that at first Lucy didn't notice. Then, when she moved her head, she felt something tickling. She put her hand up for a scratch and, to her horror, felt something furry moving across her shoulders.

She opened her mouth and SCREAMED!

All the other customers in the shop turned round and stared at the little group from Redwood School. Mr Page and Mrs Farmer came rushing over.

"What's wrong?" demanded Mr Page.

Mrs Farmer was embarrassed that it was her daughter who had caused the commotion.

"Something ran across my shoulders," said Lucy and gave a big shudder.

Darren hadn't expected Lucy to make such a fuss. "It's only my gerbil," he said scornfully. "You shouldn't have shouted like that! You could have frightened it."

He quickly grabbed his pet and put it back into his blazer pocket. "It wouldn't have hurt her," he assured Mr Page. "It wasn't causing any trouble."

"No, but *you* were!" replied Mr Page sternly. "Didn't I tell you not to bring that gerbil into school?"

Darren was quick to defend himself. "But I didn't!" he declared. "I kept it in the shed in the playground while we were at Assembly. I didn't take it into *school* at all. But you didn't say I shouldn't take it into a *bookshop*. I didn't know you wouldn't want me to do that."

Mr Page's face began to go redder and redder. But with the sales assistants and the other customers looking on, he didn't want to draw any more attention to themselves. "Go straight back into the minibus and wait there with Mr Bragg until we've finished choosing the books," he ordered. Then he added, "If I ever catch you with that gerbil again, I shall CONFISCATE it!"

Darren quickly rushed away from Mr Page. He didn't mind quite so much for himself, but he certainly didn't want his gerbil to get into any more trouble.

Chapter 5

TWO WEEKS LATER, great changes had
been made to the empty room upstairs.
Mr Bragg had given it a fresh coat of
paint before fixing up the bookshelves.
There were small tables and chairs
grouped round the room and there were
some wooden boxes containing index
cards on a stand by the window. The
new books from Applegate Bookshop
had been delivered and they—together
with all the old books—had been catalogued and arranged on the shelves.

Although Mrs Farmer and Mrs Henderson had been helping, most of the
work had been done by Miss Edwards.

She knew exactly how to organise a school library.

All the books had to have typed index cards giving the author's name and the title. In addition, some of the books had to have an extra card giving the subject. To make it easier for the children to find what they wanted, Miss Edwards was planning to put small coloured labels on the thin back end of each book.

All the story books were going to

have red labels, all the animal books blue labels, all the handicraft books green labels, all the poetry books yellow labels . . . and so on.

This was the only job that still had to be done.

Miss Edwards knew it wouldn't take her long and she planned to do this herself the day before the library was to be opened officially. Class Three had a double games lesson that afternoon, so she decided she would complete the work while they were all out in the playground.

During dinner-break, Miss Edwards went to her desk to collect the coloured labels. There was no one in the classroom and she sat down on her chair and put her head in her hands.

She had had a headache all morning and now felt a bit dizzy.

Just at that moment, Mr Page came into the room. He knew that Miss Edwards was putting the finishing touches to the new library that afternoon and he wondered if she would like some help.

He had quite a shock when he saw the supply teacher sitting with her elbows on her desk, resting her head in her hands.

"What's the matter, Miss Edwards?" he asked in alarm. "Aren't you well?"

Miss Edwards looked at him. Her

face was burning and she thought she might have a temperature. "I just feel a bit cold," she said in a weak voice.

"You look extremely hot!" declared Mr Page. "I think you'd better go home straight away. If you've got flu, you should be in bed."

"But what about the coloured labels for the library books?" asked Miss Edwards. "I was going to stick them on this afternoon."

"I'll phone Mrs Farmer and Mrs Henderson right away. They'll be pleased to do it for you," replied the headmaster briskly. "Don't worry. I'm sure they'll be able to cope."

Miss Edwards went to the staff room for her coat. On her way out of school, she passed Darren, Mike and Jim.

They were surprised to see Miss Edwards hurrying away.

"Lucky you!" said Jim. "Can we go home, too?"

Miss Edwards managed a feeble smile. "I'm not feeling very well," she explained.

Not long ago, Darren had had chicken pox. His symptoms were still fresh in his memory. "Have you got any spots?" he enquired with interest.

Miss Edwards didn't seem to take this in. "Oh dear," she said in a worried voice. "I forgot to tell Mr Page that the coloured labels that have to be stuck on the side of each library book are in an envelope in my desk."

"We'll tell Mr Page for you," said Mike helpfully.

Darren felt very sorry for Miss Edwards. He knew just how bad she must be feeling. "We'll find him right away," he promised.

Miss Edwards gave them a grateful smile. She was glad she could slip away without looking for Mr Page. She knew she could rely on the boys to pass on her message.

Darren, Mike and Jim went straight to Mr Page's room and knocked loudly on the door.

Just then, Mr Page's secretary walked by. "You won't find Mr Page there," she said. "He is showing some new parents round the school. In fact, he's busy all afternoon. Can I help instead?"

The boys looked at each other. They hadn't foreseen this difficulty.

"No, thanks," said Darren after a moment's thought. "It doesn't matter. We can manage without him."

Mr Page's secretary was puzzled but

before she could ask any more questions, the boys rushed away.

Back in their classroom, they wondered what they should do. Lucy, Sarah and Jyoti were also there so they told them the problem.

Miss Edwards was very ill—with chicken pox, according to Darren; with a cold, according to Mike; with overwork, according to Jim, who thought he continually suffered from this complaint.

"It doesn't matter what's wrong with her," said Sarah, who could be very practical when the occasion arose. "What *does* matter is that we get these coloured labels stuck on the books."

"We can ask my mum," suggested Lucy. "*She'll* be glad to help Miss Edwards."

"Well, so will *we*!" replied Darren immediately.

From her first day at Redwood, Miss Edwards had never been short of helpers. She was not only pretty but was also lots of fun and everyone in the class wanted to be her favourite.

Mike agreed with him. "It won't take us long to stick on the labels. Let's go upstairs now. There's still half an hour's break. By the time Mr Page has finished with the new parents, it'll all be done and he'll be really pleased with us . . . for a change!"

Lucy insisted on going up with the boys. "It was my mum's idea we should have a library and I want to do the labels. Sarah and Jyoti might as well come too, then we'll be finished sooner."

They found the coloured labels in the envelope in Miss Edwards' desk. Two minutes later, they were all upstairs in the library.

"Which colour labels shall we use?" asked Sarah.

Darren and Mike looked puzzled. They hadn't thought of this.

Jim was anxious to get the job done quickly. He didn't want to miss any of the double games lesson that followed dinner-break. "Let's choose our favourite colour. Miss Edwards won't mind."

This seemed a good idea so they all

set to work. For quite a while they scarcely spoke. They were so busy sticking on the labels and they wanted to be careful not to miss out any of the books.

It took longer than they had expected but at last they finished. They stood back and surveyed their work with satisfaction. Every single book had a label neatly stuck on its side.

They all felt extremely pleased with themselves.

They had done exactly what Miss Edwards had wanted . . . without having to bother either Mr Page or Lucy's mum.

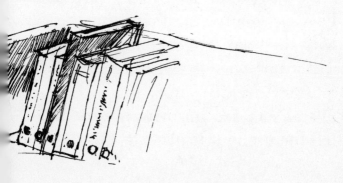

Chapter 6

MR PAGE ALWAYS enjoyed showing new parents round Redwood and today was no exception. He was proud of the school, with its light, airy classrooms, large Assembly Hall and sparkling canteen.

The four parents he was taking round at the moment were most interested in everything they saw. They asked Mr Page so many questions that he was with them far longer than he intended.

As time was getting short, the headmaster decided not to take them upstairs to see the new library but to tell them about it instead. On the spur

of the moment, he invited them to the party which the P.T.A. had arranged to celebrate the opening of the library.

"We should be pleased if you would join us for coffee and biscuits tomorrow evening at 8 o'clock," he said. "Our guest of honour will be Miss Breedy, the chairman of the Education Department of the local council. As well as most of the teachers, a large number of parents will be there, including Mrs Farmer whose suggestion it was that we should have a proper library. We are hoping that Miss Edwards will be able to come, too. She is the supply teacher who has been helping us during Miss Wilson's absence. Miss Edwards has done a tremendous amount of work getting the library organised. Unfortunately, she didn't seem at all well this afternoon so I sent her home."

The new parents readily accepted Mr Page's invitation. They wanted to see the new library and they were also glad to be able to meet some of the other parents and teachers.

Early the following morning, Miss Edwards phoned Mr Page. She said she was very sorry but she wouldn't be able to come to the party because she had the flu.

Mr Page was sorry, too. It meant he would have to take Class Three for the day. He was also extremely worried.

Last time Miss Breedy visited the school, there had been a disaster. She had been invited to enjoy a school dinner at a time when the local council was thinking of closing Redwood's canteen. However, the children from Class Three who had been helping (or who had been meant to help) mixed up the food and made Miss Breedy feel sick.

Naturally Mr Page wanted to make sure that there wouldn't be the slightest hitch on her return visit.

He knew Miss Edwards had done so much work for the new library and she was obviously the best person to explain things to Miss Breedy.

Mrs Farmer and Mrs Henderson did their best to reassure him.

"We know ALL about the library and we can explain EVERYTHING to Miss Breedy and the other visitors," said Mrs Farmer.

"We can assure you that absolutely nothing can possibly go wrong," added Mrs Henderson.

Despite this, Mr Page spent most of the day worrying.

Once the party began, however, the headmaster began to relax. Everything seemed to be going well and all the

guests were obviously enjoying themselves.

The parents had set out the refresh-
ments on large tables in the Assembly
Hall, and as people came in they were
given a cup of tea or coffee and home-
made cakes and biscuits. They stood
around chatting to each other as they
waited for the guest of honour to arrive.

At last Miss Breedy walked in. Mr Page rushed forward to greet her.

Miss Breedy had had a busy day and had gone without her evening meal so that she would be on time for the school party. She was extremely glad to see there was so much to eat and drink, and she stood for quite a while close to the refreshment table while members of the P.T.A. plied her with food.

At last Miss Breedy had had enough. She put her cup down, opened her handbag and got out her glasses and some notes. She then made a nice speech in which she said it was a great achievement for Redwood to have financed its own library. She went on to say that, on behalf of the council, she wished to congratulate everyone involved and to thank them most heartily.

Then all the visitors trooped upstairs, with Mr Page leading the way.

Mrs Farmer was waiting at the library door. Although she was sorry Miss Edwards was ill, she was delighted that she had been asked to explain to Miss Breedy how all the books had been catalogued.

"We have divided the library into different sections," she said proudly.

Mrs Farmer then pointed to the book-shelves lining the walls. "Over here, we have books on animals, next to them we have handicraft books, then there are poetry books, and in the far corner we have story books . . . and so on. Now, on the board by the door, you will see the list of subjects. Next to each subject, there is a large coloured circle.

"To help our young readers find the books they want, Miss Edwards has put a small coloured circle on each one. For example you will see on the board, there is a large blue circle next to the subject Animals. If you look at the books in the shelves, you will see that all the books about animals have a small blue sticker on the side . . ."

Suddenly Mr Page's face went bright red. Mrs Farmer had just said that *Miss Edwards* had put on the stickers. He

turned to Mrs Henderson and in an agitated voice said, "Why did Mrs Farmer say that *Miss Edwards* put on the coloured stickers? I telephoned you yesterday afternoon to tell you that Miss Edwards had gone home and you said that *you* and *Mrs Farmer* would do it."

It was Mrs Henderson's turn to look hot and bothered. "I phoned Mrs Farmer immediately after your call. She

was out, so I came straight up to the school. When I got there, I found all the stickers had already been put on the books. I assumed that Miss Edwards had managed to do it before she went home, so I didn't bother to phone Mrs Farmer."

One of the new parents who had been specially invited by Mr Page was examining the books. "That's funny," he said in a puzzled way. "According to the large circle on the board, all the books on animals should have small blue stickers . . . but this one has a red one . . . and this one has a yellow one . . . yet they're both about animals."

Mrs Farmer came over to Mr Page. "I can't understand it," she said. "The story books should all have red labels—but they haven't! Some are blue, some are green and some are yellow. I don't know what Miss Edwards could have been thinking of when she did the stickers. They've all been put on wrong."

Miss Breedy's keen ears missed nothing. "What's all this about Miss Edwards and the stickers?" she asked.

Standing together in a little group near the window were some mothers and fathers whose children were in Class Three. They looked at each other uneasily.

After school the day before, Darren, Mike, Jim, Sarah and Jyoti had told their parents how they had helped put the stickers on the library books because Miss Edwards had gone home early.

Suddenly a look of horror came over Mrs Farmer's face. At breakfast, Lucy had said she had helped Darren and his friends sort things out for Miss Edwards. She didn't say exactly what she had done . . . only that her mum would have a nice surprise when she saw the library that evening!

Mrs Drake nudged her husband. "You'd better own up," she whispered to him.

Mr Drake cleared his throat. "Er . . . er . . . I think there has been a mix-up!"

"Not again, surely!" snapped Miss Breedy.

Then Mr Page's secretary remembered how Darren and his friends had been searching for the headmaster yesterday. "Oh, dear," she said. "I might be partly to blame."

Mr Page stared at her in amazement. His secretary was most reliable and hard-working and *never* made mistakes.

Looking more than a little embarrassed, his secretary explained that she had told the children that Mr Page was too busy to see them.

Mr Drake immediately jumped to his son's defence. "There you are, you see! Obviously Darren and the gang did what they thought was best. They wanted to help, but they knew they couldn't trouble Mr Page."

"Exactly!" said Mrs Farmer, nodding heartily.

Mike Sinclair's dad gave a little laugh. "You can't say they don't try!"

There were several chuckles from some of the other parents whose children were not in Class Three.

Mr Page was in a quandary. It was one thing to be cross with Class Three . . . it was quite another to be cross with their parents! He turned to Miss Breedy and said weakly, "I am so sorry there has been another mix-up . . ." His voice tailed away.

Then, to his relief, Miss Breedy

smiled. She had had so many cups of
coffee and so many cakes and biscuits
that she was in the best of humours.
"Don't worry, Mr Page," she replied.
"Mistakes do happen."

"I promise you," said Mr Page
solemnly, "that next time you visit us,
nothing will go wrong."

Miss Breedy looked at him in a funny
sort of way. It was obvious that she
wasn't quite so sure.

Chapter 7

THE FOLLOWING MONDAY, Darren, Mike and Jim raced each other into school ... but once they were in the entrance hall, they had a surprise. There was Miss Wilson, standing talking to some of the other teachers.

Immediately the boys slowed down and walked at a snail's pace along the corridor to their classroom.

After Assembly, Miss Wilson wanted to know how they had got on during her absence.

Class Three showed her their books and their paintings and Miss Wilson was full of admiration.

"You've certainly been working hard," she said. "Now, tell me about the new library. I hear everyone in the school helped to get things organised. What exactly did *you* do?"

To her surprise, no one spoke. Miss Wilson noticed that Darren and his gang exchanged glances. She asked a few questions and was surprised at their hesitant replies.

At mid-morning break, Miss Wilson went to see Mr Page. "The supply teacher has done a good job with my class," she said. "They all liked Miss Edwards. Did she manage to keep Darren and his friends out of trouble?"

Mr Page said nothing. He just gave a strange snort.

Miss Wilson looked at him. "Was it all quiet while I was away?" she asked.

Mr Page gave another snort . . . this time a much louder one. He leaned back in his chair and spread out his arms.

A strange look came over his face as he replied. "You ask me if it was all

quiet with Darren and his friends while you were away. REALLY, MISS WILSON, YOU MUST BE JOKING!"

The headmaster's face was going a vivid shade of red. Miss Wilson decided she should quickly change the conversation. "I must say I enjoyed the computer course," she said, hoping to take his mind off his troubles.

Mr Page's eyes lit up.

"It was MOST interesting," went on Miss Wilson enthusiastically. "I'd no idea how helpful computers can be. For instance, we could have used one in our library. These modern computers prevent mistakes." Miss Wilson suspected—quite rightly—that there had been some trouble over the library—although she did not know exactly what.

Mr Page looked thoughtful. He knew

Redwood School was about to have a new computer. "I'm not sure," he said, half-serious, half-joking, "that even the most modern computer would be a match for Darren and his gang. However, our new computer arrives next term . . . so we shall just have to wait and see!"